Incy Wincy spider

Kate Toms

make
believe
ideas

Incy Wincy Spider

went UP the water spout.

DOWN came the rain,

and washed the spider OUT.

Out came the SUN

and dried up all the rain,

so Incy Wincy Spider

climbed up the spout again.

Here we go again!

But why does **INCY** climb the **spout?**

(In case you are in any doubt.)

Because he's **SPUN** his web up **high,**

so he can **see** the **world** go by...

(It's easy **dropping** to the floor,

but climbing **UP** is quite a chore.)

Incy Wincy Spider

doesn't like the rain,

he's got his swimming goggles on,

(he won't get
caught again).

But ... just as he starts climbing

UP the water spout,

another shower of rain falls down

and

washes

Incy

out!

Uh-oh!

Now **Incy's** trying once again,

umbrella **at the ready,**

the **rain** won't beat him **this** time

if he takes it

nice and **steady.**

There **has** to be

another way

to get home on a

rainy day!

Looking round, what's INCY seen?

A round and bouncy trampoline!

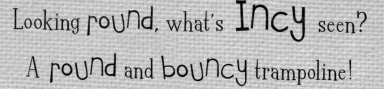

Wheeeee!

He's found a way to get home fast ...

but bounces high
and flies straight past ...

Not again!

Over the hedge,

over the wall,

a **stripy** tent

breaks his **fall**.

Looking **puzzled**,

Incy thinks.

He rubs his **hairy head** and **blinks**.

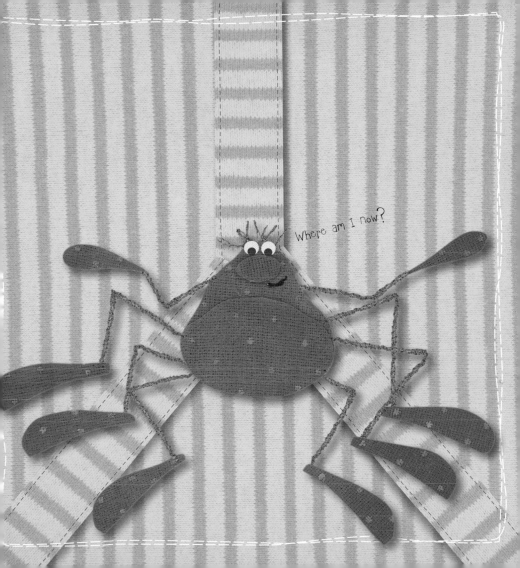

Where am I now?

The **washing's** out

the **weather's** fine,

Incy wobbles on the line,

when suddenly
a breezy breeze
blows Incy to some nearby trees.

Through the leaves,

INCY spies

several pairs of

beady eyes.

"But **WORSE** than that,"

INCY squeaks,

Incy's running, quite puffed out,

but in the distance,

sees the

spout.

It's the best idea
he's had all day.

He'll climb the spout another way.

The rain comes dow

nside the spout,

so he'll climb UP

not in, but out!

Back in his **web**,

he's **HAPPY** now.

(It's easy when you've worked out how . . .)

The lesson **learned?**
Try, try again . . .

and don't be put off by the rain!

Home at last!

So Incy Wincy Spider

can climb the water spout.

And even if the rain pours down,

it can't wash Incy out.

For Incy Wincy Spider

has found another way,

and now it's "easy-peasy"